First published in the United States 1990 by Dutton Children's Books, a division of
Penguin Books USA Inc.

Originally published in Great Britain 1989 by Andersen Press Ltd., 62-65 Chandos
Place, London WC2. Published in Australia by Century Hutchinson Australia Pty.
Ltd., 89-91 Albion Street, Surry Hills, NSW 2010. Colour separated by Photolitho
AG Offsetreproduktionen, Gossau, Zürich. Printed in Italy by Grafiche AZ, Verona.

ISBN: 0-525-44600-1   First American Edition   10 9 8 7 6 5 4 3 2 1 0

EARTH HOUNDS
as explained by
Professor Xargle

Translated into Human by Jeanne Willis
Pictures by Tony Ross

E. P. Dutton · New York

Good morning, class.

Today we are going to learn about Earth Hounds.

Earth Hounds have tusks in the front and a waggler at the back.

To find the tusks, dangle a sausage at each end.

Earth Hounds have buttons for eyes, a sniffer with
two holes, and a built-in necktie. They use their
necktie to lick their underbellies and also

the icicle cups of Earthlets who are not looking.

Earth Hounds can stand on four legs, three legs, and two legs. They can jump as high as a roast beef.

For dinner, they consume wigglemeat, skeleton
biscuits, a flying snow muffin,

a helping of living room rug, and a sock that is four days old.

After this feast they must be taken to a place called
walkies, which has many steel trees.

The Earth Hound is attached to a string so that he can be pulled along in a sitting position.

In the park the Earthling finds a piece of tree and
hurls it back and forth.
The Earth Hound is made to fetch it.

Then the Earthling takes a bouncing rubber sphere and flings it into the pond.

Now the Earthling must fetch it.

On the way home, the Earth Hound rolls in the plop
of a moohorn.

He arrives back at the Earth Dwelling with stinkfur and rests under the bed covering of the Earthling.

Here are some phrases I want you to learn:

"Where is Rover?"
"Have the pipes backed up?"
"Either he goes or I do!"

Earth Hounds hate the hot water bowl. They tuck their wagglers between their legs and make a *Wooo-Woooooo* noise.

Once free, they dry themselves on piles of compost.

Here is a baby Earth Hound, or Houndlet, asleep in the nocturnal footwear of an Earthling.

The Earthling has placed many newspapers on the floor for the Houndlet to read.

That is the end of today's lesson.

If you are all very good, we will visit Planet Earth to play with a real Houndlet.

Those of you who would like to bring your own pets along should sit at the back of the spaceship.